Fairies
Magic
B

Illustrated by
Ela Jarazbek

Designed by
Brenda Cole

To stop water
from seeping through to
the next page, unfold the flap
at the back of the book and
place it under the page you're
about to work on.

Dip the brush into
water, then brush it
across the black patterns
and lines within each
shape to see the paint
magically appear.